# How Do You Sleep?

by **Louise Bonnett-Rampersaud**

illustrated by **Kristin Kest**

Marshall Cavendish Children

Text copyright © 2005 by Louise Bonnett-Rampersaud
Illustrations copyright © 2005 by Kristin Kest
All rights reserved
Marshall Cavendish, 99 White Plains Road, Tarrytown, NY 10591
www.marshallcavendish.us

Library of Congress Cataloging-in-Publication Data
Bonnett-Rampersaud, Louise.
How do you sleep?/by Louise Bonnet-Rampersaud.
p. cm.
ISBN 0-7614-5231-1
1. Sleep—Juvenile literature. I. Title.
QP425.B66 2005
573.8'68—dc22
2004025517

The text of this book is set in Berling.
The illustrations are rendered in oil paint on paper.
Book design by Virginia Pope.

Printed in China
First edition

1  3  5  6  4  2

*To my family* —L. B-R.

*To Claire and Grandmom Kate, with gratitude* —K. K.

Little bird, little bird, in your nest,
how do you like to get your rest?

I gather some twigs,
and branches and leaves,
and snuggle, snuggle down
in the cool, cool breeze.

Big bear, big bear,
    how do you sleep,
all winter long
    without a peep?

I nibble
  nibble munch
for the long
  winter haul,
then I curl up
  in my cave
in a great bear ball.

Horsey, horsey,
on the farm,
how do you sleep
down in the barn?

Inside my stall
all full of hay,
I stand and
dream the night away.

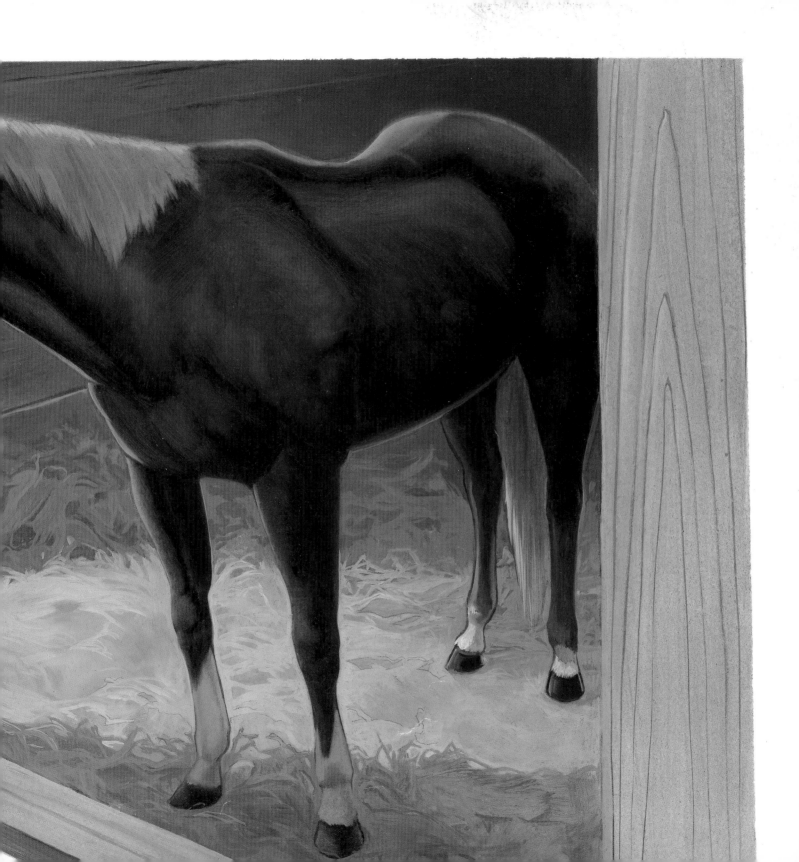

Little pig, little pig,
beneath the sky,
how do you sleep in
your piggy sty?

I oink and I grunt,
spread my hooves
   just right,
then I dream
   dreamy dreams
as my eyes shut tight.

Green frog, green frog,
how do you sleep,
out in the middle of
the pond so deep?

With a hippity-hop
and a splish, splash, soak,
I leap to my lily pad,
ribbit, ribbit, croak.

Bunny rabbit, bunny rabbit,
deep underground,
how do you sleep when
the moon comes 'round?

I chomp on
my carrot
with a crunch,
crunch, bite,
then I tunnel
down my hole
where I'm safe
for the night.

Children, children,
by your beds,
how do you rest your
sleepy heads?

Down under covers
tucked in tight,
we listen to
our stories
in the glowing
moonlight.

We wiggle and we wriggle
'til we're cozy—just right,
then it's cuddles, dreams and kisses
for a long, safe night.